We Had a Picnic This Sunday Past

We Had a Picnic

Jacqueline Woodson

Hyperion Paperbacks for Children
New York

This Sunday Past

Illustrated by **Diane Greenseid**

First Jump at the Sun/Hyperion Paperbacks edition, 2007

3 5 7 9 10 8 6 4 2

Printed in Singapore

Library of Congress Cataloging-in-Publication Data on file.

ISBN-13: 978-1-4231-0681-4
ISBN-10: 1-4231-0681-4

Visit www.jumpatthesun.com

For Kali, Sadie Rain, and Madeline Ivy
—J.W.

For Phyllis and the
Hamilton High School Babies
—D.G.

Grandma wore her
blue dress
with all those flowers on it.
Brought biscuits and chicken
and me.

Everything she made a big show of putting out. Got up at four this morning to make this chicken. Best batch I ever fried. These biscuits just as tasty. Can't chew for swallowing, can hardly swallow 'cause you'll be too busy reaching for more. And look at my grand-child. Just as pretty as a day. Turn and show them that dress I made you, Teeka. Oh, how Grandma can brag when she wants to. Then turning to me she whispered,

H ope Martha don't bring that pie again. Everyone says that pie's a bit on the dry side, but not in front of Cousin Martha, 'cause that would hurt her feelings. Grandma says Martha should be in any room but the kitchen. Says she thinks Cousin Martha scares the stove into baking bad.

Every year, same Cousin Martha, same dried-out apple pie. And you better eat every bite of it so you don't hurt Martha's feelings.

uther is Grandma's oldest boy. He married Lucinda. Now they have Terrance, mean old cousin of mine. Terrance brought plastic flies, put them right on Auntie Sadie's sweet cob corn. Goodness, can my Auntie Sadie scream!

And give an ear a pinch if it needs one.

And whisper to Grandma, **You seen hide or hair of Martha's pie?**

Uncle Luther
set a loaf of
cinnamon bread in the
center of things.
Grandma, smiling just as proud, said,

Can't my boy bake himself some bread!

Look at my second cousin Laurie's son, Jefferson.
He thinks he's so cute. **Humph!**

Auntie Kim's my all-time favorite.
She's the smart one—teaches second
grade, I whispered to Paulette.
(Paulette's no relation—just my best friend.)
Don't go bragging, Grandma said, nudging
me. But you can tell she's just as proud.

Auntie Kim doesn't want to marry (and
maybe me and Paulette won't, either).
I brought some cranberry muffins,
Auntie Kim said, **and cookies
shaped like angels for my angel,**
handing one right
to me.

Then Cousin Trevor came—
empty-handed.
Pretty-boy Trevor walking
into that park with a handful
of nothing.
Can't eat air, I whispered
to Paulette.
Don't be a smartie,
Grandma said, but you know
she was thinking the same
exact thing. Cousin Trevor
picked daisies as he
strutted up, talking
about daisies
for all the
pretty ladies.

Hmph,
Grandma said,
frowning.
Hmph, me and
Paulette
echoed.

Still no sign of Cousin Martha. Still no sign of that pie.

Moon Pie and Callie—Moon Pie is really Joseph, but don't he look just like a Moon Pie?—came empty-handed, too. Nobody can eat that smile you brought for the camera, Moon Pie.

 ister Carol and Reverend Luke toted the Bible to the picnic.
Reverend Luke can eat like the devil—strange, since he's
such a holy man.

   Little Astrid, two front teeth missing, trailed behind
them carrying a pail of peaches fresh as summer.

Tooth fairy bring you anything? Paulette wanted to know.
Got a quarter for them, Astrid said, and held out his hand to
show us the shiny quarter there.

hen Mr. Pete came running—
he's got a thing for Grandma.
Mr. Pete, well, you can set
that sweet-potato pie right
over here by me, I said.

Wasn't that peach cobbler Miss
Mary's daughter Pat brought
just out of this world?

And yams and potato
salad and collards, a big
old ham, Grandma's
chicken fried crisp
and tender, melt-in-
your-mouth
cornbread . . .

hen here came Cousin Martha with a big pink box out in front of her, just as proud, smiling.

Goodness, Grandma whispered, don't tell me she made **two** this year.

No time to bake, Martha said.

Store-bought cake and my apologies.

Oh, but Cousin Martha, Grandma said, all year long, I've been thinking about your pie.

Goodness,
that picnic table was
something to see!
Topped it all off with cookies, melon,
homemade ice cream, and the most
delicious store-bought cake
Cousin Martha **never** made.

We had a picnic this Sunday past.

You should have been there.